# California Diaries #4

# Amalia

## Ann M. Martin

SCHOLASTIC INC.
New York  Toronto  London  Auckland  Sydney

*Interior illustrations*
*by*
*Stieg Retlin*

No part of this publication may be reproduced in whole or in part, or stored in a retrieval system, or transmitted in any form or by any means, electronic, mechanical, photocopying, recording, or otherwise, without written permission of the publisher. For information regarding permission, write to Scholastic Inc., Attention: Permissions Department, 555 Broadway, New York, NY 10012.

ISBN 0-590-29838-0

Copyright © 1997 by Ann M. Martin.
All rights reserved. Published by Scholastic Inc.
CALIFORNIA DIARIES is a trademark of Scholastic Inc.

12 11 10 9 8 7 6 5                                    0 1/0 2/0

Printed in the U.S.A.                                    40

First Scholastic printing, December 1997

*The author gratefully acknowledges
Peter Lerangis
for his help in
preparing this manuscript.*

# Amalia

A
Vargas
Family
Christmas
Palo City, California

Art: Amalia Vargas
Ink: Amalia Vargas
Text: Amalia Vargas
Any resemblance to persons, alive or dead, is definitely, absolutely, on purpose.

12/20

Yo, Notebook.
Merry almost Xmas.
At least <u>you</u> listen to me.


Sun 12/21

Dear Nbook,
   I will never ≡V≡R leave you out in
plain sight again. Not after today.
   <u>Isabel, if you are reading this, you</u>
<u>are the witch sister of Christmas</u>
<u>Present and I hope you melt into the</u>
<u>carpet with Big Tooth Lover Boy</u>
<u>standing over you and crying his guts</u>
<u>out.</u>
   I have been writing in you since
September, Nbook. You and I both
know this hasn't been easy. I hate
writing, so I draw a lot. And everything
I write is so POLIT≡.
   No more. It's time to say what's on
my mind.
   I mean, we're all home today and

everybody's having a good time —
Christmas, happy happy, whatever. I'm
in my room, wrapping presents I
bought for Mami and Papi. And Isabel
barges in without knocking. And where
are you, Nbook? Faceup on my bed,
where I've left you.

"Cute," says Isabel. "You can
write?"

I am boiling inside. But you know
me, Nbook. I always keep cool. "It's
mostly drawings," I say. "Keep your
hands off."

Does Isabel listen? No. She never
listens. She just <u>has</u> to open you up.
To the Christmas picture. She sees
the drawing of her and Big Tooth
Lover Boy. Only Simon's teeth don't show
because he's kissing her in the picture.

Now she wants to kill me.

I ask you, is this fair?

I will never understand my big
sister. To me, she's Dr. Jekyll. (Or is it
Mr. Hyde? Anyway, the bad one.) To
the rest of the world, she's Saint
Isabel of the Lost Causes.

She gets Christmas cards from her old teachers in San Diego. (Do I? No. My teachers are thrilled that I moved.) She's constantly bringing home gifts from the women's shelter where she works. "One of the residents gave this to me," she says. "Just a little something for the holiday."

I want to give Isabel a little something for the holiday. A bonk over the head.

These journals are supposed to be _private_.

Which brings me to another point. No offense, Nbook, but why did we have to move to a place where the schools _force_ you to write journals? We didn't _have_ to write journals in San Diego.

Some of my classmates have been doing this since first grade. To them it's, like, ho hum, another five pages.

To me, it's torture. Already my fingers are cramping.

The worst part is, it's totally _pointless_, since the teachers are never ever going to collect it.

So why do I open up my inner thoughts to my nosy sister who everybody loves even though she's a thief who <u>steals my private property</u>?

I know why.

Because, Nbook, you are very cool.

But from now on, you stay under my mattress.

Fa la la la la, la la la la.

Sun night, 12/21

Maggie is rich. Not just in the way of a big house and nice stuff, but Major Money.

I mean, I've always sort of known this about Maggie. People drop hints. But I've never thought much about it one way or another. What's inside a person is what counts. Inside, Maggie is friendly and talented and unsnobby.

Tonight, Nbook, I see the outside for the first time.

I'm at the Blumes' for dinner. Dawn and Sunny are there too. The house is at the top of this canyon. It's so high up you look <u>down</u> into the smog. The backyard looks like they imported a small Hawaiian island and plopped it right there. The pool is <u>huge</u>.

We sit down to eat, and the plates look so expensive I'm afraid to touch them. But it doesn't matter because the maid takes them away and serves dinner on different plates anyway. Which seems weird to me but I don't say anything.

The maid's name is Pilar and she's Latina. Maggie says she's studying to be an actress. I wonder if she's acting when she smiles at everybody and takes orders from Mr. and Mrs. Blume.

The main course is this shrimp dish

that's about the most delicious thing I've ever eaten. So I do the polite thing and compliment the Blumes on their cooking.

Well, Mrs. Blume gives me this funny, tight-lipped smile. Mr. Blume laughs and says, "It's catered." And I feel like melting into the Persian rug.

Don't worry, Nbook. Things loosen up eventually, and I end up having a good time.

But now I have a new problem. My Christmas list. My belated procrastinator's Christmas list that I shouldn't even be thinking about anymore.

Over dinner, as I listen carefully to the conversation, I pick up what people want to receive. Which is helpful in some ways, but not in others.

Okay, here's the whole thing, with my changes added (including people who weren't at dinner):

<u>Revised Christmas Shopping List</u>

<u>Saint Isabel</u> (who I overhear telling Big Tooth Lover Boy she'll "die" if anyone gives her another sweater) — Return sweater. Buy earrings. Or maybe a bag of coal.

<u>Cece</u> — Hair stuff.

<u>Marina</u> — Science fiction book, not related to <u>Star Wars</u> or <u>Star Trek</u>. (Does that leave <u>anything?</u>)

<u>Maggie</u> — Oh, just something that the daughter of Hayden Blume the gazillionaire movie producer might <u>not</u> have. Like maybe her own private village.

<u>Dawn and Sunny</u> — ????? <u>Gift</u> friends or <u>nongift</u> friends?

<u>James</u> — ????? <u>Boyfriend</u> gift (cologne)? Or <u>friend</u> friend gift (new shades)?

To be decided by <u>tomorrow</u>!

¡ SURPRISE !

Hey, Nbook. Bet you didn't expect to see me here.

Thank sunny.

She says she writes in her journal during her study hall. Everyone thinks she's really working.

I say, great idea.

Besides, today is the Useless School Day of the Year. Vacation starts tomorrow, so we have to be in school for <u>one day</u> this week. Of course, practically no one is here, and I don't blame them. Vacation should have started on Friday!

Boy, do I need to vent.

It's <u>three days before Christmas</u>, and I am like a flea on a sweaty dog. I can't stop jumping.

Remember my plans? All changed.

This morning, I'm at my locker, and I'm thinking: cologne. For James's gift, I mean. Mainly because the stuff he wears is so awful. So what if he thinks we're boyfriend — girlfriend? I'll deal with it.

Besides, we probably <u>are</u>. I look for him every day before and after school. And I always feel so good when we're together in the hallways. James has really changed my life. Before I met him, I felt so <u>small</u>. Moving into a new city and school was hard enough. But did I know that the Vista eighth-graders would be going to the high school building this year? No. All of a sudden, I'm not only a new student but <u>also</u> in the youngest class. Then I meet James, and all of a sudden upper-graders are talking to me.

He's cute. He's talented. His guitar playing is amazing. Besides, would I be managing the rock group of a guy who was <u>not</u> a boyfriend? I think not. Would I hold hands with a <u>friend</u> friend? Would I have kissed him 2 times? (Maybe 3.)

So I'm kind of in a trance at my

locker, thinking about all this and deciding James _must_ be a boyfriend.

Then he walks up to me.

Does he say "Hi" or "Good morning" or even "Merry Christmas"?

No. The first words out of his mouth are "Vanish rehearsal. Tomorrow."

"Excuse me?" I say.

He repeats himself, slowly, as if I had a brain transfer with a toad this morning.

Here's the problem, Nbook. When something like this happens, my mind goes all weird on me. The words flood into my head right away. I _know_ just what to say. I _know_ I should tell him it's crazy to have a rehearsal three days before Christmas and I have a thousand presents to buy including his and I cannot make it, no way no how, proceed without me.

But something happens to the words on the way from my brain to my mouth. They fall apart. They trip over each other. I start to speak and I sound like a total _idiot_.

"I don't know. . . ." I say.

"We need you to listen to the instrumentals," James barges on. "Maggie can't be there to sing."

<u>Of course not</u>, I want to say. <u>She's shopping like any other normal person.</u>

How that transformed into "Okay, I guess," I will never know.

But it did.

And I am stuck.




Tues 12/23
4:3¢

Nbook old buddy,

I am sitting in the backseat of Simon's car. He and Saint Isabel are giggling away in the front.

We are all going shopping, then Simon is going to drive me to rehearsal.

I have decided he is a nice guy. I shouldn't call him Big Tooth Lover Boy. Saint Isabel, however, is still in the doghouse.

And, you, Nbook, are helping me make her very paranoid.

Sometimes I am <u>such</u> a bad sister.

12/23
bedtime

I must be crazy.

I must be totally out of my mind.

I race through the Vista Hills Mall at warp speed. I look at every science fiction book ever written, smell every men's cologne ever made, nearly die standing in long lines, then make Simon drive me to the Vanish rehearsal. I arrive about ten minutes late, which usually counts as <u>early</u> to these guys, and — surprise surprise — they've already started playing.

Justin Randall is sitting there, so I sit next to him. I say a few words to him, like, "I can't believe there's another fool here 2 days before Christmas."

He laughs, we chat a little while. The music sounds pretty good, and I'm feeling exhausted but great because I've <u>almost finished my shopping</u>.

I smile at James, but he's deep into his guitar.

When the group breaks, I walk up to James. He's still deep into <u>something</u>, I can't tell what, because he's not looking at me.

"Sounds great," I say.

He gives kind of a half grunt, half laugh. "You heard it?"

I figure he didn't see me come in. "I was right here."

"I know. But you looked like you had something else on your mind."

<u>What is he talking about?</u> I'm saying to myself. I must have seemed totally out of it.

I mutter something like, "Well, it's kind of a busy time."

And then I see James glaring at Justin.

<u>Blink!</u> goes the light in my head.

I realize what's going on. <u>He thinks I'm flirting with Justin Randall!</u>

Please. Like I'm really interested in stealing the guy that Maggie is interested in, right in front of the whole group, in her absence. Like I'm hopelessly boy-crazed and can't help myself.

I can't even convince myself to be interested in James!

Anyway, the idea is so ridiculous, I start to laugh.

Big mistake. If looks were knives, I'd be dead. "What's so funny?" James asks.

"Nothing," I say.

"You think this is a joke?"

"No!"

"Are you laughing at me?"

I control myself. I try to explain. I try to tell him the concept of me liking Justin is silly, but it comes out all wrong. It sounds like I'm telling him <u>he's</u> silly. He just gets madder and madder.

Finally he stomps away.

I'm standing there, suddenly alone and totally embarrassed. Everyone else is trying to pretend that they haven't heard every single word.

And I'm thinking, I broke my back today for <u>this</u>?

Tomorrow I am taking back that cologne. Christmas Eve or no Christmas Eve.

I changed my mind, Nbook. Again.

I know, you think I'm stupid. But I can explain.

It starts this morning, just after breakfast.

Marina calls me. The first thing she says is, "My brother can be a real jerk." She says she's yelled at James for embarrassing me. She told him he should call me. Basically, she's apologizing for him.

I'm still mad at him, but I tell Marina my mind is open.

I know Simon and Isabel are going last-minute shopping. I decide that if James calls before they leave, I won't return the cologne.

But he doesn't call.

Soon Simon and Isabel are leaving. I have the cologne in my hand, gift-wrapped and ready for return, and I ask if I can go along. Isabel asks why.

I try to explain. I don't want to

make a big deal out of it, but nothing I'm saying is making much sense. Isabel keeps asking questions, and finally she gets me to pour out everything I'm feeling about James.

"Sounds like a misunderstanding," Simon says. "Why don't you call him?"

"He should call me!" I reply.

Isabel nods. She says James was wrong to fly off the handle.

I admit that some of it is my fault. That I wasn't really making myself clear to him. That maybe I made things worse by saying the wrong things.

Isabel thinks about this for a minute. Then she asks if I like James.

"Yes. I mean no," I reply. "I mean, as a friend, at least. Maybe more. I'm not sure. I like his sister. And I like being with him a lot. Sometimes. Maybe I should give him something that's less . . . romantic or personal or whatever." (Speak much, Vargas?)

Simon smiles. "Cologne is safe," he

says. "Isabel bought me cologne when we were just friends."

"Yeah, and look at you now!" I answer back.

Simon and Isabel grin at each other. Isabel rests her head on his shoulder.

"It wasn't the gift of cologne that did it," Simon says. "I didn't really like the smell anyway."

Isabel acts all shocked and they get into a make-believe fight that ends in a laugh and a kiss.

Another public kissyface scene between the Saint and the Teeth.

Only this time, Nbook, I don't feel like puking.

Instead I'm looking at them and thinking: This is a relationship.

And I'm wondering if James and I will ever be that way. I mean, it must be nice to care about somebody so much, and to know he feels that way about you too.

A question occurs to me, so I blurt out: "Did you guys fight a lot when you first met?"

Simon grimaced. "All the time, until she got used to me."

I think about this. Then I decide to stick with the cologne.

But now Simon and Isabel are both insisting I come shopping with them anyway. Just to cheer me up.

I agree, and off we go.

Well, the mall is a madhouse, of course. A kid almost knocks me over on the escalator. I stand in humongous lines again and buy some cool CDs. (I'll give them to Dawn and Sunny if they buy me presents. If they don't, the CDs are mine.)

We spend way too much time in there, and I am in a foul mood on the way home.

"Hey, where's your Christmas spirit?" Simon asks.

"Stuck somewhere between electronics and ladies' lingerie," I snap.

Then, completely out of nowhere, Isabel asks me the strangest question. Do I want to go with her to the women's shelter?

I tell her she may be dumb enough to work on Christmas Eve, but why should I tag along? Only I say it in much nicer words.

Isabel gives Simon a look, then smiles at me. "You said you wanted to experience Christmas spirit."

Nice try, but no go. Simon drops me off at home, I put on some Christmas CDs, and Mami puts me to work.

Around dinnertime I take a break and call James. (Yes, Nbook. The silence was killing me.)

He apologizes for blowing up at me. He tells me he understands what happened now; he "had it out" with Justin.

(Nbook, have you ever noticed that girls "talk it out" but boys "have it out"? What does this mean?)

Anyway, I invite him to come over tomorrow. He says he and Marina are going to their grandparents', but they'll be back at night. Which is fine, because my relatives will be gone by then.

He sounds excited.

I wonder what he's giving me for christmas.

I know, Nbook, I know. I mustn't be greedy.

Well, the house looks beautiful. The food is arranged in the fridge, so we can put it all together tomorrow.

And I am going to bed.

Good night.

Ho ho ho.

Thursday December 25

¡ FELIZ NAVIDAD !

I love my new dress from Mami and Papi.

I love my CDs from Isabel.

I love my savings bond from Tio Luis the Banker.

<u>And I had so much fun with my cousins!</u> Why can't they all live closer? (I know why. Because WE moved!)

I would like to say gracias, gracias to everyone for all the gifts of the day, which are too numerous to mention. But you know who you are.

I am in hiding up here in my room because my stomach is so bloated from eating and laughing and talking nonstop that I am in mortal danger of making embarrassing noises in public.

You don't mind, do you, Nbook?

# AMALIA'S CHRISTMAS

BEFORE    AFTER

Maggie came over this afternoon. Mami kept offering her food, but she wouldn't eat <u>one thing</u>. I don't know how she does it.

Maybe I should ask her to give me lessons.

Or maybe not. I loved every morsel. And Maggie could stand to put on a few pounds, in my opinion, anyway.

So, while I am digesting, I will listen to music and tell you all about today.

At 5:57 A.M. Isabel and I run downstairs. (Actually we were both up at 5:3φ, but we restrained ourselves.) Mami and Papi drag themselves out of bed, complaining but smiling. We turn on the radio and every station is playing Christmas music.

Then, after we finish opening presents, Papi starts making his patented huevos rancheros, and Isabel runs upstairs to get dressed. She says she is going to the shelter.

"On <u>Christmas</u>?" I blurt out.

"Yup. Want to come?"

Crazy. Right, Nbook?

Now, here's the weird thing. I don't know what it is — maybe the carols on the radio, maybe the presents, maybe the smell of breakfast and the feeling of being together and happy at our first Palo City Christmas — but I call out, "Okay!" Just like that.

I actually <u>want</u>, in my heart, to be with my sister.

Big Tooth Lover Boy shows up and gives Isabel a necklace. Then — I cannot believe my eyes — he gives presents to Mami and Papi. I mean, really. This is like something from an old movie.

Papi asks if Simon is trying to hint at something, which embarrasses Simon and Isabel and they both laugh too hard. Then Mami winks at me and says, "Good thing you're going along, Amalia. You'll make sure they behave."

Now I'm embarrassed too. As Simon, Isabel, and I leave, our faces look like red peppers.

Anyway, I guess I'm expecting this women's shelter to look like a church or a school with a lawn or something. But it is nothing like that. Simon drives clear across Palo City to a funky area I've never been to.

Isabel tells me the shelter is called GAEA. "Gaea" is the name in

Greek mythology for the goddess of the earth.

I ask Isabel if Mami and Papi know she works in a neighborhood like this.

She shakes her head and says, "It's really nice inside."

Which is true. The lobby looks like this big, comfortable living room. I see a Christmas tree, a menorah, a Kwanzaa kinara, and a creche.

Right away I understand why some of the presents are wrapped in baby paper. All over the place I see

Oops. Gotta go. The doorbell rang. Must be James.

12/25
later

Yup. James.

He is all sweetness.

I give him the cologne.

He gives me a present too. I rip it open right there.

It's an ankle bracelet. With my name and his. Linked together.

Whoa.

I will not stress.

I will enjoy my presents. I will go with my family to visit Abuela Aurora at the nursing home near San Clemente.

I will not think about James.

I will not think about what his present means.

I will not wear it either, until I know where we stand.

Period.

Nbook, please. You <u>must</u> remind me when I leave off in the middle of a story. I can't remember <u>everything</u> by myself.

I know, I know. I told you I hate writing.

But we're amigas now. In a big way. I can tell you stuff and I don't get all tongue-tied.

Finger-tied.

Whatever.

Okay, where were we? Flashback to Christmas Day. GAEA. Big Tooth Lover Boy drops off me and Isabel. We're lugging bags of presents into the building, and all of a sudden little kids are running around me like I'm Santa Claus.

Their parents are in the lobby, which spills into a corridor that branches off in either direction. They are chatting away, smiling at the kids or scolding them. The kids try to be polite, but it's hard.

It feels like a big PTA event. Except for one thing. None of the parents are dads. Not one. They're all mothers. Latina, white, African-American, Indian, Asian. A world festival.

Even Santa Claus is a woman.

She's performing magic tricks in a corner.

Many of the moms are thanking Isabel for coming. They're introducing themselves to me and shaking my hand. But I'm so busy with the presents and the kids that none of their names stick in my head.

And all the while I'm realizing I have never really talked to Isabel about this place. "Women's shelter" — what does that mean anyway? <u>Homeless</u> women?

Some of these women look pretty well off. Beautiful clothes, done-up hair, and nice nails. What are they doing here?

As I'm trying to put the presents under the tree, I hear someone talking to Isabel. "Two of our child-care people aren't coming today," she says. "Would you mind helping with the little ones?"

I hear Isabel answer, "But Ms. Hardwick wanted me to help with the food and punch."

Well, the kids are so cute, and I'm tickling one of them who has a laugh like Porky Pig, and I'm having the best time. . . .

It happens again, Nbook. I speak right up without even thinking. "I will!"

Of course, right away I'm saying to myself, <u>It's Christmas Day, and you're going to baby-sit for 3φ screaming kids you've never met before?</u>

A smiling African-American woman shakes my hand and says, "Thank you so much. Your parents are blessed to have daughters like you two. I'm Ms. Hardwick, and I'm the director here."

Now the Santa is passing out presents. The kids are ripping off the wrapping paper and screaming with delight.

Ms. Hardwick introduces me to two other girls, about Isabel's age, named Lori and Jenna. They're volunteers too, and they're going to help baby-sit.

We all go down the corridor, along with a couple of moms, to the center's playroom. Behind us I hear sound effects: spaceships swooping, lasers buzzing, cars racing, dolls talking to each other in squeaky voices.

The playroom is pretty small, and many of the toys and games are broken and old, but the kids are too busy playing with their gifts to notice.

Actually, the baby-sitting turns out to be pretty easy. I make a friend, a boy who just turned three, named Mikey. He keeps saying, "You my mommy" to me. He doesn't say much more than that, and he can't seem to leave my side. We play "space fighters," using two action figures called Max Endor and Mr. Peebles.

When it's time to leave, he starts throwing things and crying. I try to stop him, but it's impossible.

Finally Ms. Hardwick picks him up. "Maybe Amalia will come back," she says to Mikey.

"Mommy come back?" he says.

This is weird. What can I say?

"Sure," is the first word that comes out of my mouth.

Nbook, I will never learn my lesson. Now I <u>have</u> to return to GA≡A.

Maybe not. Kids forget. Don't they?

James is being so nice to me. Today he's wearing the cologne I gave him, which is a big step up from his dad's ancient bottle of Old Spice — which must have been left over from his college days, because it is beginning to smell more like Old Mice.

As for the ankle bracelet, well, I just don't know what to do, Nbook.

I don't want to wear it just because James wants me to. That's not right. Being a girlfriend isn't like doing homework. It's not an assignment. Right?

Right.

So anyway, today we go to see <u>Fatal Judgment</u>, which I've seen already at Maggie's house because her dad produced it. The only reason

I'm seeing it again is because James insisted.

And who is right in front of us in line but

Sunny is cool. She's wearing about a half dozen studs in her ears. When she turns at a certain angle, her midriff shows under her shirt, and if I'm not mistaken, she has a pierced navel.

I am dying to know how she convinced her parents to let her do that (if she <u>did</u> convince them).

Well, she starts talking. And talking. And talking. About the movie, her Christmas gifts, her mom's cancer, her dad's bookstore, all in a big tumble of words. She leaves out a few key details, so you <u>have</u> to listen, just to understand what she means.

No one minds the blabbering. Even though some of her news is so sad, her delivery is hilarious. We're all laughing.

I wish I could talk like that. She expresses more in two minutes than I do in two hours.

"Uh, Sunny? Time-out?" Ducky finally says. "Maybe some other people would like to talk?"

I finally speak up. I try to describe my experience at GAEA, but even though I think it's interesting, I somehow seem to drag the conversation down.

At one point James nudges me and says, "Show them the ankle bracelet."

Moment of truth. I tell him I left it at home.

He doesn't seem too thrilled. But he doesn't make a big deal about it.

In fact, he doesn't make a big deal about anything. He doesn't talk much before the film. He doesn't say anything during the film. And after the film, when Ducky suggests we all go out for a snack, he says, "I have to go home and practice."

So we all say good-bye, and Ducky and Sunny go off to Tico's Tacos.

James is silent as we walk to his car. I assume he's sulking about the ankle bracelet. But I'm not sure. So I try to make conversation. "Did you like the movie?" I ask.

He shrugs. Then he says, "Are they, like, you know . . . going out?"

"Sunny and Ducky? I don't know. I think they're just friends."

We're at the car now, and James gives me this funny smile. "That's what I figured."

"Why?" I ask.

He kind of snickers to himself. Then he says, "I just don't think Ducky's her type, if you know what I mean."

Which seems strange to me, because Ducky's cool and funny and outgoing, just like Sunny. "Well, I can see what they like about each other," I remark.

We climb into the car, and James starts up the engine. All the while he still has this little smirk on his face. I ask him what he's thinking about, but he says never mind and changes the subject.

We start talking about the movie. He doesn't understand some of the plot, which _is_ pretty confusing, but I explain it to him because Maggie has explained it to me.

Mostly, though, James wants to talk about Jennifer McBride, the star. He asks if I've ever met her at Maggie's house.

"No, but I bet _you'd_ like to," I say.

"I just like the way her hair looks," James says.

I start laughing.

"I'm serious," James says. "_You_ should get your hair cut like hers. You'd look much better."

"Thanks a lot! I mean, really. You're comparing me to the most gorgeous actress in the world. I could never look like that."

James smiles. "No. You could look better than that."

Is that corny or what?

But I like the way it sounds.

I like it a lot.

Thursday January 1!!!!!

1/1

12:09 in the afternoon

Don't give me that blank, surprised look, Nbook.

Yes, I just woke up.

No, I have never slept so late in my life.

I have never stayed up so late in my life either. Until after 3:00! I can't believe Papi and Mami let me. I guess 13 is the magic age. (It

probably helps that they were invited
to Rico's house last night. And that
practically everyone else's parents
were there too.)

## What a Party!

First of all, everyone shows up. All
my favorite people. I have the best
time getting to know Dawn and Sunny a
little more. We're all singing our brains
out and eating like pigs. And somehow
I find time to draw a portrait of the
scene.

At midnight, everyone starts singing
"Auld Lang Syne," but James and his
friends don't know how to play it. They
try to fake it, and it sounds horrible,
but nobody cares.

After the song, James lifts me in
the air and gives me a big kiss. Right
on the lips, right in front of the whole
party.

I'm a little embarrassed but not
really. Everyone's acting kind of wild.

The Chavezes put on a tape, a
dance mix. James and I are forehead
to forehead, slow dancing even though

the music is loud and fast. James is smiling. I can tell people are staring at us. It all feels great.

"It's a beautiful night," James says. "Want to go outside?"

I say yes, and we walk out into Rico's backyard. From all around the neighborhood we hear yelling and music and noisemakers. A cool breeze makes me shiver, and James holds me tight. I smell lemons in the air, from the trees in the yard. A few lights are blinking above, and I'm trying to figure out if they're stars or airplanes.

Then I can't see them anymore because James's face is in the way. He pulls me close and kisses me. I can tell he wants to <u>really</u> kiss me, <u>deep</u> kiss me. Then I remember the funniest thing: Dr. Scott examining my teeth and saying, "Did you know that jaw muscles are among the strongest in the human body?" (Is this weird or what, Nbook? I'm outside alone with a guy on a crisp night, and I think about my dentist?)

Anyway, Dr. Scott is right. I have no trouble keeping my jaw closed. The kiss, to tell the truth, is pretty wonderful anyway. But I start feeling self-conscious so I pull away. I mean, come on. Mami and Papi are right inside. Besides, I am not ready for that kind of kissing. First things first. Let's get past the ankle bracelet dilemma.

James pulls away. He's smiling, but he looks a little puzzled. "Is this all right?" he asks.

"Is what?" I ask back.

"You know . . . sneaking outside?"

I nod. "Yeah."

We stand there, silent, for awhile. Then James says it.

"You know, I really love you."

I cannot believe this. I am stunned. So I just say, "Huh?"

"I said, I — I like you a lot," James replies. His voice sounds nervous and I can feel he's shaking a little.

Now, maybe my ears are playing

tricks, but I know — I <u>know</u>, Nbook —
that he did not say <u>like</u>.

But I take his word for it. "I like
you too, James," I say.

We stare into the sky, and I'm
thinking, <u>what next?</u> when we hear a
car horn blaring in the driveway.

Caught in the headlights! Just like
a Hayden Blume movie. James puts his
hands in the air and says, "Don't
shoot!"

It's the Blumes, who've come to
pick up Maggie. Well, <u>they're</u> not
driving, their chauffeur is. Which is
good, because neither of them looks in
any condition to drive. Especially Mrs.
Blume, who can barely walk. She
comes out of the car, wobbles a
little, holds on to the roof ledge, and
calls out to us, "Uh-uh-uh! Inducent
piblic display of afflection!"

James shoots me a look. I can tell
he's about to laugh.

We follow the Blumes inside into
the garage. Mrs. B is slurring her
words, and I'm worrying the whole

time that she's going to blow chunks
all over the floor.

Poor Maggie. She looks embarrassed
as she says her good-byes. But we
all act as if nothing's wrong.

After that, the party spirit is kind
of spoiled. But it's late, and we're all
exhausted anyway.

People start going home. Everyone
makes me promise to send copies of
my portrait. I say good-bye to Justin,
who's there with his parents. Then
Ducky starts kissing all the girls and
saying dramatic farewells. He's driven
to the party alone because his
parents are overseas on business and
his older brother went to a different
party. When he reaches me, he thinks
he's morphed into Fred Astaire and
starts swinging me around the garage,
singing "Auld Lang Syne."

We're all laughing as Ducky breaks
away and dances off by himself,
blowing more kisses. The Big Exit. That
is _so_ Ducky.

I see Mami and Papi are already

putting on their jackets. Mami says she's concerned about Isabel, who has gone to a party at Big Tooth Lover Boy's house. So we say a quick round of thank yous and we head for the door.

James is busy putting away equipment. As I walk up to him and say good-bye, he picks up an amp and walks toward the back of the garage. He looks up, grunts "'Bye," and disappears.

Oh, well. I'll call him today.

1/1
8:φφ P.M.

Nbook, Nbook, I don't know what to do.

Isabel won't stop crying.

Just a little while ago, we're all in a great mood. We're in the kitchen, preparing dinner. Papi is playing one of his old beloved Tito Puente tapes and we're dancing and laughing.

And then the phone rings. Mami puts her hand on the receiver and tells me to turn the music down.

I run into the living room and turn the volume knob. I hear Mami saying "Happy New Year" to someone, and then "Yes, Isabel's right here."

When I get back into the kitchen, Isabel is sitting at the desk, the receiver cradled to her ear. Her mouth is open and her eyes are filling with tears. Then she puts the receiver on the desk and runs upstairs. Obviously she's continuing the phone conversation in Mami and Papi's room because she calls down, "Hang up now, _please_!"

As Mami obeys, I ask if Simon was the one who called. I figure he and Isabel had a fight.

Mami shakes her head. "It wasn't Simon. It was Ms. Hardwick."

Well, the Tito Puente tape ends and no one bothers to turn it over. Isabel comes downstairs and her makeup is all wiped off. I can tell she's been crying. But when Papi asks if she's all right, she nods and says, "It's nothing."

Mami, Papi, and I keep asking her what's the matter. Is someone sick? Did someone die? Was Isabel fired? (Can you be fired from a volunteer job?)

Finally Isabel says, "Something happened at GAEA, that's all. To one of the residents."

"<u>What</u> happened?" Mami insists. "Tell us, hija!"

Isabel just shakes her head. "I can't."

She hasn't said a word more about it all night, Nbook. And now she's sobbing in her room.

What am I supposed to do?

Fri 1/2

You know what I wish, Nbook? I wish I could close my eyes, go back to sleep, and wake up this morning again.

This year is not off to a good start.

I'm in my room, trying to relax, and all I hear is Isabel. She's muttering to herself. She's clacking her rosary beads. She's typing something on her computer. She's whimpering.

I finally go into her room. She's sitting at her desk, and her fingers are flying across the keyboard.

I see the words "Dear Linda" at the top of the screen.

Linda.

I'm trying to think who that is. I'm running through the faces of the moms I met at GA≡A.

"Hi," I say. "Who's Linda?"

Isabel whirls around, like I'm some masked intruder. "Who said you could come in here?"

"Sorry," I reply. "Must have forgotten my invitation."

I mean that as a joke, but Isabel sure doesn't take it that way. She's sitting in a strange position, with her head covering the screen so I can't see it. "Get out of here!" she yells.

This gets me angry. I've been worrying and worrying. All I want to do is help. And when I reach out, Isabel pushes me away.

"I already saw the name," I say. "You're writing to Linda. Who's that?"

I try to look around her, but Isabel now drapes a magazine over the monitor, so it covers the screen. "Amalia, I am not allowed to talk about anyone in the shelter. You know that."

"But I volunteered there," I remind her.

"For a day! You're not officially signed up."

I sit on the bed. "Isabel, I met some of those people. Don't you think I care about them too? You're not the only one with a heart in this family!"

Isabel looks like she's going to cry again. Immediately I feel bad. I start to apologize, but Isabel cuts me off.

"When you volunteer at GA≡A," she says, "you have to sign this confidentiality statement. You're not supposed to find out residents' last names, just first names. And you're even discouraged from mentioning <u>those</u> outside the center. It's to protect their identities."

"Protect against what? Organized crime or something?"

Isabel shakes her head. "Their husbands. Their boyfriends."

Now it sinks in. I think about TV movies and news reports. About dysfunctional families and battered women. And then I remember Mr. and Mrs. Parkinson in San Diego, how, in the months before they split up, we would hear their screaming fights all the way down the block.

"That bad, huh?" I ask. "I mean, with Linda?"

Isabel's forehead wrinkles up and a tear rolls down her cheek. I put my arm around her shoulder and say, "Look, I don't know who Linda is. I have no idea what she looks like. And I'm not going to go blabbing her name all around town. Won't you feel better if you talk to someone about this?"

Isabel thinks for a moment. Then she nods. "Yesterday one of the residents left the center. She told Ms. Hardwick she was going to stay with her family in Anaheim. Well, her family was there waiting. But so was her ex-husband. He'd found out where she was going. And . . . "

My stomach is churning. I say to myself, <u>Linda must be alive. Isabel is writing to her.</u>

The first question I can think to ask is, "Will Linda be able to come back to the shelter?"

Isabel nods. "When she's out of the hospital. I guess the ex-husband doesn't know about GAΞA. But it's not only Linda I'm worried about. It's her little boy. He's still at the shelter."

I think about all the little kids I met. I ask Isabel which boy it was.

"His name's Mikey," she replies.

Sorry about all the wet spots, Nbook. It's been a long, emotional night.

I spend all this time comforting Isabel, then I go to bed myself and — ZING! — I'm a basket case. I can't stop picturing that poor little boy.

I think about how he called <u>me</u> Mommy. Why? Where was Linda that day?

Finally, around midnight, I can't stand it any longer. I know it's late but I have to talk to someone. So I call Maggie's private number.

Maggie sounds practically dead. But when she hears me crying, she wakes right up.

I tell her everything, taking care not to mention names. Maggie listens carefully and makes two suggestions.

1. I should go to sleep. 2. I should write to Mikey. Something creative, something that would make him happy.

He probably needs all the support he can get.

It's late. Too late. But I have to work on 2.

Yo, Nbook. Here I am at a vanish rehearsal. I am listening to "Fallen Angel" for about the tenth time, and I'm bored.

James is mad at me again. I do not understand him.

About a half hour ago, I'm showing Maggie the comic strip I drew. She's not really getting it. I explain that Max and Mr. Peebles are Mikey's action figures.

But Maggie is such a <u>writer</u>. She writes these meaningful poems and songs, and she thinks everything has to have hidden meanings and deep thoughts.

"But what does the story <u>mean</u>?" she asks. "How does it end? How is it supposed to make him feel better?"

What I want to say is this: When I was playing with Mikey, I noticed how great he felt whenever Max triumphed. So Mikey identifies with Max.

Now that Mikey must be feeling scared and vulnerable, I figure he'd like to see a comic strip in which Max saves the kids in the center.

That's what I want to say. But what comes out is something like this: "See, Mikey's Max and Mikey's scared but Max is strong and saving people, so Mikey might feel that way too."

Of course, Maggie looks at me as if I'm speaking a foreign language. So I try to explain. Then James walks into rehearsal and suddenly I'm all distracted. I can see he's looking at my ankle. Checking to see if I'm wearing his bracelet.

I'm not, and he doesn't look too happy about it. Now he's looking over my shoulder. "What's that?" he says.

Well, I'm feeling bad enough that I showed the drawing to Maggie. I'm already coming close to breaking my promise to Isabel. So I close you right up, Nbook, and I put you in my backpack. "Just a drawing. It's nothing."

He looks totally insulted. "If it's nothing, why can't your boyfriend see it?"

Your boyfriend. He announces it aloud like that, so everyone can hear.

"Later, maybe," I say.

"Is it something about me?" James asks.

Maggie laughs at this. "No, James. It's about a younger guy."

At that point, Rico starts yelling at us because he wants to start rehearsal.

James grabs his guitar, Maggie gets behind the keyboard, and the band starts playing "Fallen Angel."

I wish Maggie hadn't said that.

James looks like he wants to throw his guitar at me.

Nbook, why is life so <u>complicated</u>?

I do not understand guys. I never will.

<u>Never!</u>

Okay. Let me start from the top.

Rico calls a break in the middle of rehearsal. Everybody heads to the table, where there are soft drinks and snacks.

Except James. He walks outside.

I know he's mad, so I follow him. Soon we're out of sight of the garage door, and James stops walking. "Hi," I say.

He whirls around. "Don't you ever treat me like that," he says.

"Like <u>what</u>?" I reply.

"Like, make fun of me."

"I wasn't making fun of you!"

"Yeah? Well, what's in your pocket?"

I am so angry and frustrated, I pull you out, Nbook. I flip to the Max Endor drawing and shove it toward him. "There. Read it!" I snap. "It's what Maggie and I were talking about."

"It's, like, a comic strip." He looks closely at it. "It's good."

I grab it out of his hand. "Are you happy now?"

"Sorry, Amalia. I just thought you were keeping secrets from me."

"Even if I <u>was</u>, so what?" I'm almost shouting now. "Do you have to know everything about me?"

"I said I'm sorry." James tries to put his arm around me. "How come you never told me you were so talented?"

He's smiling at me, but now <u>I'm</u> furious. "You think you can make everything better, just by complimenting me?"

"Whoa. Come on, Amalia, it's not such a big deal."

"Like, I'm so in love with you I'll let you insult me and be suspicious and accuse me of being in love with everybody in the world and insult my friends and then expect me to forgive you and act like I'm your girlfriend? Why? Just because you're sixteen?"

"Uh, slow down," James says. "What

are you saying? You're <u>not</u> my girlfriend?"

My jaw is hanging open, Nbook. It's like he hasn't heard <u>one word</u> of what I've said.

"Stick to girls your own age," I mutter.

I turn. Then I walk around the garage, around the house, and all the way to the corner gas station, where I call home.

A few minutes later, Isabel picks me up. I am crying and she asks why.

I tell her I've broken up with a guy who wasn't even really my boyfriend.

1st draft, letter to James

This is Amalia. She is feeling pretty embarrassed. She just did something really stupid.

This is James. He doesn't know what happened. He was just being himself, and Amalia started yelling at him, then walked away.

James is wondering what is going

through Amalia's mind. He's wondering why she didn't speak to him in school today. And why she hasn't called him. Maybe he's a little angry too.

Well, Amalia doesn't blame him. And she would like to call. But she knows she will not find the right words to say. She will open up her mouth and start another argument.

See, Amalia's pretty confused too. She likes James a lot. She thinks he's cute. She loves the way he plays guitar. She wants to go out with him and get to know him more.

But James does a few things she wishes he wouldn't do. Like <u>assume</u> she's his girlfriend. And get mad at her for talking to other guys. And be suspicious of her for the most harmless, innocent things.

Amalia doesn't want to be James's enemy. She still hopes they can talk things out.

Can they?

Amalia hopes James will answer soon.

# Amalia's Dream

Mami says dreams are really messages from your subconscious. They're about the unsettled things in your life. Even if they don't seem like they are.

Well, Nbook, this dream is pretty obvious. Mikey is on my mind.

When I head downstairs for breakfast, I'm going to tell Isabel I have made a decision.

Tomorrow, after school, when she goes to GAEA, I'm going to go with her. To officially sign up.


1/6
8:34 P.M.

My mind is spinning, Nbook. I don't know how I can write about everything that happened today.

First of all, I'm walking up the school steps and James is standing against a pillar, talking to Rico. He turns toward me with no expression on his face. Like he doesn't know me.

I say hello, take out the letter I wrote, and hand it to him. Then I go to my locker.

I see him once during the day. After lunch he walks up to me and says, "I'll drive you home today."

Not a question. A statement.

I'm happy about this but a little nervous. I tell Maggie about it at our lockers, after last period. She looks really worried and volunteers to go with me in James's car. Sort of like a chaperone. I think it's silly but she insists.

Maggie and I walk out of school together. At the curb, James is holding open the passenger door of his car. I ask if we can give Maggie a ride, but he shakes his head. "It's personal," he says.

We leave her standing on the sidewalk, looking worried.

James turns on a tape. He doesn't say a word as he pulls onto Las Palmas Drive.

And he passes right by Royal Lane, instead of turning toward my house.

"James, that was my block," I remind him gently.

"I know," he says.

Soon we're at Las Palmas County Park. He pulls into a space in a deserted part of the parking lot.

Next thing I know, we're walking among the trees. I have never been to this place before. In the distance I hear children's voices, but where we are, it is pretty deserted. We follow a nature path and end up by a pond. In the middle of the pond is a small island, and by its shore a couple of turtles are basking in the sun. James throws a rock at one of them, and it quickly pulls back its head.

James laughs and throws another rock. He thinks this is <u>funny</u>. I am starting to feel edgy.

I try to make myself comfortable. I take in the scenery. I turn toward the sun. I listen to the birds.

Without looking at me, James points to a grassy spot in the shade. "Sit."

I sit down. James is pacing now, fumbling for something in his back pocket. He pulls out a crumpled-up sheet of paper. As he unfolds it, I realize it's my note to him.

"I read this," he says.

I gulp. "Uh-huh?"

"You're a really good artist."

"Thanks. But what did you think about the words?"

"I was confused — you know, the way you write <u>James</u> and <u>Amalia</u> instead of <u>me</u> and <u>you</u>. That was a style, I guess." James turns to me now. His brow is all scrunched up. "But I'm . . . happy. I — I thought I'd lost you."

Right away my heart melts. "You were worried?"

"Me? No way!" James looks away

and sighs. "Well, yeah, I guess. Maybe. Sorry."

"Don't be sorry. It's . . . nice. It shows you like me. You want to work things out."

James's face reddens. He exhales deeply, then throws another rock at the turtle island. For a long time he says nothing.

I try to make conversation, but James is in another world. Finally he sits down near me. His body's facing mine, but he's looking at the ground.

When he gazes up, his eyes are moist. "Amalia, I know this sounds weird, but . . ."

His voice trails off.

"But what?" I ask.

"But . . . I really like you. I was trying to tell you that at the New Year's party."

"Well, I like you too, James —"

"No, I _really_ like you. I mean . . . like no one else. Ever. In my whole life."

I am stunned. All I can say is, "What?"

"I know. You can't believe it. I can't either. I mean, I _can_, but it's weird —I shouldn't feel — a guy my age —"

My tension is lifting. James is tripping over his words. He's so unlike his confident self.

He's sounding like me.

All I want to do is comfort him. I stand up and reach my arms out.

Next thing I know we're embracing, rocking back and forth. His face is buried in my shoulder.

"I don't think it's weird at all," I say softly. "I mean, we're only three years apart, James."

"And I'm the one acting like a little kid," James mumbles. "Sorry I got so suspicious. I guess it was because of that ankle bracelet. When I saw you weren't wearing it, something just snapped, I guess. I didn't even think it would be that important to me. But it was."

He pulls away from my shoulder and I see tears in his eyes.

I smile. "So, I guess that means you want us to work it out, huh?"

James doesn't answer. Not with words, at least. He just leans toward me.

I close my eyes, and we kiss.

I don't know how long it lasts. All I know is that it feels way too brief.

When it's over, I'm feeling light-headed and happy. Now it's my turn to bury my head in his shoulder.

"I think about you all the time, Amalia," James says, almost in a whisper. "I'll do anything to keep you in my life. Anything."

Wed 1/7
study hall

I was a fool, Nbook.
A total fool.
James is the sweetest guy.

As we drive home from the park,
he sings to me. Then he promises he
will pick me up for the next day of
school (today).

Later, he calls me just to ask how
dinner was.

This morning, he calls before he
leaves to make sure I'm ready to go.

(Isabel thinks this is all hilarious.
She calls him James the Puppydog.
Which, I suppose, is better than Big
Tooth Lover Boy.)

Anyway, he shows up on time,
blowing his horn and waking up the
whole neighborhood.

I run outside. I have long pants on,

to cover up the ankle bracelet I am wearing. I want to surprise him.

As I climb into the car, I cross my legs so the bracelet shows. He is so busy singing along to a tape, he doesn't notice the bracelet until we're at a stoplight. Then he does this huge double take.

He lets out a whoop, then leans over and wraps me in a hug.

Soon the cars behind us are blowing their horns. James breaks away, leans out the window, and shouts, "Yo, blow it out your ears!"

He leans on his own horn, and he keeps leaning on it as he drives toward school.

I know I should be embarrassed, but I'm not. I'm laughing.

We park, then walk into school, arm in arm. Inside, he kisses me good-bye and runs off to his locker.

I spot Marina on the way to my locker. She winks and we exchange a high sign.

Maggie, Dawn, and Sunny are

staring at me as if I just arrived on a flying carpet.

"Uh, I guess you patched things up?" Maggie asks.

"You could say that," I reply.

They bombard me with questions, and I tell them as much as I can before homeroom.

All day long I'm flying. I am missing James and counting the minutes until we see each other.

Before study hall, I open my locker and find this note stuck into the vent:

AMALIA!

Hi. I miss you! Beach after school? Just for a walk.

See ya
—J.

Why why why WHY WHY did I promise Isabel I'd go to GA≡A today??????

Can I back out of it?

Okay, Nbook. Who do I let down? James or Mikey?

Am on my way to GA≡A. James
seemed pretty annoyed. But I think
he understands.

The moment I walk into the center, I know I'm in trouble.

I hear a bloodcurdling scream from somewhere inside the building. Ms. Hardwick is yelling, "Mikey, what is <u>wrong</u> with you?"

I can't see what's happening, but I hear footsteps clatter away down the hallway.

An assistant named Lila smiles at Isabel and me. "I'll take you to the nursery."

We follow Lila down the hall. A dozen or so kids are in the nursery with a few moms and staff workers. They're all grateful to see us.

I play with the kids, but I can't stop thinking of Mikey and hoping he shows up.

Then I see Max Endor. He's on the floor by the window. His legs and one of his arms have been ripped off, and his costume is shredded. His eyes have been blackened in with markers.

Ms. Hardwick finally comes back. She has a clipboard with some forms I need to fill out.

As I take it, I ask about Mikey.

Ms. Hardwick sighs. "He's having a rough time. His mom's in the hospital. There were some complications."

"Is she all right?" I ask.

"I think so. We just received news that she's due back here any day now."

"Isn't Mikey happy about that?"

"He doesn't understand, Amalia. He's frightened. At his age, a parent's absence is difficult to comprehend. One moment he's happy. The next he's impossible to handle."

"I'd love to see him."

Ms. Hardwick says she isn't sure he'll let me. He's refusing to see anyone.

I fill out my papers. By the time I'm done, Isabel is pointing at her watch and saying we have to go.

I am really sad about not seeing Mikey, but Isabel assures me we'll come back soon.

Ms. Hardwick is waiting for us in the lobby. She's looking at the wall, with a funny smile on her face.

All I see there is an empty sofa.

And then I notice the four little fingers clutching the side of it.

I peek around the back of the sofa. Mikey is huddled there, hiding.

"Hi, Mikey!" I say.

Mikey doesn't answer.

"I'm Amalia. Remember me?"

Mikey shakes his head.

I don't know what to do, so I tousle his hair.

Mikey lets out a scream. Then he lunges at me, fists flying.

"Mikey!" Ms. Hardwick yells.

But Mikey is halfway across the lobby.

He disappears down the hallway, with Ms. Hardwick in pursuit.

I want to chase after them, but Isabel's hand is on my arm. "Come on," she says. "I think we're making the situation worse."

Simon is waiting for us out front. He sees how upset I am, and he insists on driving us to Starburst's.

After a day like this, the crowded mall isn't exactly what I have in mind.

But we go. And we talk. Simon and Isabel share a huge sundae, but I have only a glass of soda. My appetite is gone.

Well, Nbook, almost a whole day
has passed since my adventure at
GA≡A. A lot has happened.

First of all, I'm eating my breakfast
this morning when Mami shuffles sleepily
into the kitchen and says, "Your
boyfriend called last night. Twice."

Isabel laughs. "The puppy is
lovesick."

I ignore her. But inside I'm feeling
great.

Anyway, James shows up promptly
in front of the house. As I walk
outside to meet him, I sense that my
older sister is jealous. Simon Big Tooth
Lover Boy does not pick her up every
day.

I am all smiles as I slide into
James's car. I say good morning and
lean over to kiss him on the cheek.

But he's already pulling away from
the curb. The tape he's playing is this

weird punkish stuff I've never heard before.

"So how was it?" he asks.

"Don't ask," I say. "Mikey is hostile."

"<u>Mikey?</u>"

"You know, the little boy I told you about?"

"Uh-huh." James speeds around a corner. The car's tires screech. "How little?"

"Three, I think. James, why are you driving so fast?"

"Three? Three times what, Amalia — six? Or does he have some special condition? Like a fast-aging gene or something, that makes him old enough to date girls?"

"James, what are you <u>talking</u> about?"

A light is turning from yellow to red. James speeds right through.

"Careful!" I scream.

"And that place you told me about," James says sarcastically, "that shelter or whatever — it doesn't happen to have round marble tables and serve ice cream, does it?"

I let these words sink in. He's describing Starburst's. "Wait. Were you at the mall last night?"

A smile creeps across James's face. "No, but <u>you</u> were. With a not-so-little boy, I hear."

I slump back into the seat. I cannot believe I am hearing this. "James, that happened to be my sister's boyfriend. My sister was there too. It was <u>after</u> we'd been to the center."

Now James is slowing to a normal speed. "Vinnie didn't tell me about another girl."

Vinnie. I vaguely remember meeting a friend of James's with that name. "So Vinnie was at the mall and he recognized me. He <u>spied</u> on me."

"I'm going to kill him," James says.

"Not if I get him first."

I am angry. I don't say another word as James pulls into the parking lot.

He gets out of the car and starts walking toward the school. I run to catch up.

I tell him I really want to talk to him. I say we've wasted the entire ride to school with a stupid argument. I wish the eleventh-graders' lunch wasn't one period after the eighth-graders', but maybe we can meet in between.

James shakes his head. He says he's going out for lunch. With some friends. Then he suggests, "You could come with us."

I laugh. "Right. And cut math?"

James shrugs. "I cut all the time. Nothing ever happens."

I say no, of course. But it's tempting.

Ducky's hanging out by the eighth-grade lockers, talking to Maggie, Sunny, and Dawn.

I'm thinking about James. About our conversation. Somehow the ride to school has left a bad taste in my mouth, and I can't figure out why.

As I'm taking my books out of my locker, Maggie is singing a new lyric she wrote for vanish.

It's absolutely beautiful. Something about a sad, lonely girl who spends her life only doing what everyone _else_ wants her to do. As I'm listening, my heart is breaking.

Maggie's songs are so personal. She's struggling, Nbook. She's really learning to break away from her Daddy's-good-little-girl image.

I wish her parents were more like Mami and Papi, who don't put too much pressure on us. Maggie may have all that money, but what's the point if she's not allowed to be herself, right?

Anyway, I'm lost in my own world when I hear Ducky mention something about tonight's rehearsal.

"Are you going, Ducky?" I ask.

"We all are," Ducky replies. "Sunny, Dawn, and me. We'll be . . . groupies!"

He shouts the word "groupies" in

this high-pitched voice that makes us all laugh.

At that moment, James walks around the corner. He's giving Ducky a wary look.

Ducky sees it and flinches.

"Yo," James calls out, gesturing to me with his head.

As I walk toward James, I hear Ducky mutter, "I should try that sometime. So much more efficient than 'Would you come here, please?'"

"<u>What was that?</u>" James snaps.

"Nothing," Ducky replies.

James starts walking toward Ducky, but I take his arm. "What's up, James?" I ask.

"You forgot your makeup," James says.

I remind him I don't wear makeup. But for some reason he's still glaring at Ducky, so I wave in James's face. Jokingly. To get his attention.

Finally James turns to me and says, "Fiesta Grill."

"Huh?" I reply.

"Meet me there. My lunch period."

I have no time to answer because the homeroom bell sounds. We all scatter.

I am a total space cadet in class, Nbook. I can't concentrate. I'm worrying about everything. Whether it's really okay to cut math. Why James is so moody. What's happening with Mikey. My school notebooks are filling up with doodles instead of classwork.

On top of that, I can't get Maggie's lyric out of my mind. I think of the sad girl in the song, the girl based on Maggie.

But it's not Maggie I'm picturing. I'm seeing someone else. Another girl who does things for others. Who thinks of herself second or third or fourth, but never first.

Someone with the initials A.V.

And I'm realizing why I feel so strange about my ride to school with James.

The fact is, he'd accused me of lying. Just like that. He heard a rumor from someone and assumed I was guilty.

I tell myself he's human. He's hotheaded. And no one is immune from jealousy.

I admit, I can be that way too. Believe me, Nbook, I have apologized my way out of plenty of situations.

The thing is, if James had apologized, I'd probably have forgiven him on the spot. But he hadn't. He hadn't said a word about it.

You weren't around when I was a little girl, Nbook. But whenever Isabel or I hurt someone's feelings, Mami always used to say, "The injuries that you can't see are the most painful."

Well, I believe that. And I think James needs to learn it too. I have to talk to him.

You know what, Nbook? I really don't need to go to math.

Here I am, after all that.
And he's not here yet.

First I should tell you, Nbook, that
he showed up.

I'm standing by the candy
machines, trying to look invisible, and I
feel this sharp tap on the shoulder.

I practically scream.

James is laughing. "What are you
doing here?" he asks.

"Waiting for you," I say.

"I mean, here at the machines.
Why didn't you sit, save us a booth?"

There's so much I want to say to
him, but people are all around us, so
I just smile and follow him to a table.

He opens a menu. "The
cheeseburgers are the best."

"Uh, James? Listen, I need to tell you something — "

"It's okay if you have no money. My treat."

"It's not that. It's — "

"Yo! Bruce! Patti! Over here!"

I turn. Bruce and Patti have just entered the grill, and they're headed our way with big smiles.

"It's what?" James asks me, distractedly.

"Nothing," I say.

Our friends sit down. Everyone orders chili dogs and cheeseburgers. They're all talking and laughing. But I'm not hungry. I hardly say a word.

A few minutes before the start of next period, we leave together. We stroll up the street. We walk into school. Mr. Schildkraut is across the hall, and James nods to him.

He waves back.

Then he squints at me.

I am such a fool, Nbook. I have totally forgotten that the eleventh-

graders are allowed to leave school —
but us eighth-graders are not.

"Amalia Vargas?" Mr. Schildkraut
calls out.

"Uh-oh," Bruce murmurs.

Mr. Schildkraut is bearing down on
me now, staring through his thick
glasses. "Am I mistaken, or are you
supposed to be in a class?"

Well, guess what, Nbook? Not even
a full semester in Vista, and I have
the very first "warning" on my record.

One more and I'm suspended.

ROOOCK A BYE BA-A-BY...

What is wrong with me, Nbook?
I cannot sleep.
I am totally wired.
Every fifteen minutes I hear the downstairs mantel clock chime. I dread it. I want to run down there and throw a rock at it.

<u>I can't stand this!</u>

I have to calm down. Sort out my thoughts.

As if school yesterday wasn't bad enough, I come home and Isabel is frantic. The moment I walk in the door she grabs my hand and says, "Let's go."

At this point, I have had enough of being bossed around. I shake her off and start to yell at her, but she stops me.

"It's Linda," she says. "She called me from a pay phone. She took a taxi to GAΞA and as it pulled up, she saw her ex-husband's car parked in front — with him in it!"

"Ohmigod. Did he try to hurt her?"

Isabel is running out the door now, and I'm following close behind. "She didn't stop," Isabel says over her shoulder. "She told the cabdriver to keep driving. But the ex-husband took off after her. The taxi driver wound around through the backstreets and lost him. But now Linda's afraid to go back to the center. She thinks he might be waiting."

"Didn't she call GA≡A?"

"Yes. She spoke to Ms. Hardwick, but the phone call was cut off."

We're in the car now. Isabel backs out of the driveway and onto the street.

I am full of anger. I want to find that guy and kill him.

Then I realize what we are doing.

"Isabel, why are _we_ going?" I shout.

"I don't know!" Isabel replies. "But we can't just sit around and do nothing. Ms. Hardwick has called the police. We're not going to be alone."

I'm hoping she's right. I'm also wondering if we ought to stop off for some bulletproof vests.

A police car is parked in front of the center. Part of me is hoping Isabel will turn around, but she pulls into the parking lot.

We run inside. The first thing I notice is that the christmas tree is now gone. The lobby feels cold and dull, like a hospital. A crowd of grown-ups, including two police officers, is gathered around the sofa.

Ms. Hardwick sees us. As she turns and heads our way, I spot a young woman on the sofa. Her arm is in a cast, and tears are running down her cheeks.

Isabel asks if Linda's okay. Ms. Hardwick exhales deeply and takes us aside. "I asked you not to come, Isabel. You could have been caught in something very ugly."

Isabel hadn't told me she'd been warned away. I'm not sure whether my sister is brave or stupid.

Ms. Hardwick explains that Linda's ex-husband, Robert, walked into the center and introduced himself with a false name. He said he was applying for a custodial job.

Linda had given Ms. Hardwick photos of Robert, which were shown to all the staff members. So the receptionist was suspicious. As she picked up the phone to call Ms. Hardwick's office, Robert walked off, saying he had to use the bathroom.

Ms. Hardwick got the call from the receptionist and the call from Linda at the same time. Right away she notified the whole staff and called the police. Everyone in the building went searching for Mikey and Robert, but they were both gone.

Finally Ms. Hardwick heard a shout from outside. A shopkeeper from across the street had noticed Robert escaping through a storage room window with Mikey.

A security guard ran outside and tried to hold Robert back, but Robert shoved him away and the guard was badly hurt. In the end, Robert escaped.

And he had Mikey with him.

My head is reeling as I hear this. "Mikey's been kidnapped," I murmur.

Ms. Hardwick nods slightly. Out of the corner of my eye, I see that Isabel is walking toward Linda.

Linda gets up from the sofa. She hugs Isabel and says, "Thanks for being there, sweetheart."

"Is there anything at all that I can do?" Isabel asks.

"The police say they'll find Mikey," Linda insists. Her voice doesn't sound too hopeful, though.

Isabel introduces me. She says that Mikey adored me.

Adored. Not adores.

I can't keep in my tears. I start weeping right there.

Linda hugs me. I'm standing there, rocking back and forth with her and feeling horrible. She's the _mom_, Nbook — her son is gone and _she's_ comforting _me_!

That doesn't last long, because Linda has to answer questions from the police.

Isabel and I linger awhile. We help take care of the kids. They're not themselves today — either spooked and withdrawn or totally wild.

The moment we leave the center,

I burst into tears again. Isabel puts her arm around me. We sit in the car for a long time in the parking lot. We try to make sense out of what happened, but it's impossible.

Over dinner, Mami tries to calm us down, but Papi is very emotional. He insists we should stay away, it's dangerous, we're taking our lives in our hands, etc., etc.

Finally the phone rings. Papi picks up.

It's James. Papi tells him we're just sitting down to dinner and I'll call him back.

That's when I realize I should be at the rehearsal right at that moment. James probably wants to know where I am.

To be continued . . .

Sorry, Nbook, but I'm yawning. I have to go to sleep. No offense, okay?

·good morning!·

Sorry if I'm scaring you, Nbook. You can't imagine what it feels like to be this tired.

The only reason I'm awake now is that Papi let me drink some coffee this morning. I'm sure I'll be a zombie again by study hall — so right now, while I have the chance, I will finish what I started yesterday.

It's after dinner. I'm clearing plates when I realize I've forgotten about the vanish rehearsal. I tell everyone I have to go.

Papi, who is still in a bad mood, starts yelling at me. He says I shouldn't be going outside while a kidnapper is on the loose. Mami calms him down, but she's not thrilled about me leaving because I have homework.

I promise to do my homework at Rico's, and Isabel agrees to drive me.

The rehearsal has already started when we arrive. Maggie is singing "Hey, Down There" as I walk in. That song is so sad. It doesn't help my gloomy frame of mind.

Dawn, Sunny, and Ducky are all there. Justin, Marina, and Cece have shown up too. I smile and chatter with them. I think I'm covering up my mood, but right away they all start asking if I'm okay.

I tell them what happened. I try to keep it brief because we're all supposed to be listening to the group. But I can't help crying.

Justin sits next to me and puts his

arm around my shoulder. The others gather around and try to comfort me.

It's a nice feeling to be surrounded by friends. I wish James were among them, though.

By the time the group takes a break, I'm a lot more relaxed. I wave to Maggie, who is working something out on the keyboard. James is unhooking his guitar. I walk up to him and apologize for showing up late.

I'm about to explain about Mikey when he walks away. Just like that. Not even a hello.

Maggie notices. "What was that all about?" she asks.

I shrug.

"YO, JUS!" James is bounding toward Justin now, greeting him at the top of his lungs. "THE BABEMASTER!"

He gives Justin a high five that would knock me off my feet.

Justin looks a little wary. "You're sounding good, James," he says.

"Hey, I have a new title for a

song!" James says, still in a loud voice. "It's based on this old saying — you know, 'when the cat's away, the mice will play'? The title is 'When the Songs Begin, the Guys Move In.' What do you think?"

"Uh, cool," Justin says.

"Maybe you could help us write it, huh? It's based on you."

Now James and Justin are face-to-face. James has that crazy look in his eye. Justin's face is hardening, like he expects a fight.

Nbook, remember when I called Isabel a Jekyll and Hyde? Cancel that comment. That description fits <u>James</u> much better.

The rest of us are standing there in shock. All except Ducky, who rushes toward James and Justin.

"Uh, guys?" Ducky says. "Look, whatever you're upset about, I'm sure we can all talk it over —"

James points a finger at Ducky. "You butt out. Since when are <u>you</u> trying to tell <u>me</u> about girls?"

"James, knock it off!" I call out. I take his arm, and Marina joins me.

Rico grabs James's other arm. "Come on, buddy."

"Justin wasn't doing anything wrong," Maggie pleads.

"He was only <u>talking</u> to me," I say.

"It's okay," Justin says. He's clenching his fists now. "I can take care of myself."

Oh, great. Rumble time. Just what I need.

Just then, a loud blast of noise makes us all jump. I scream with pain, covering my ears.

Patti is standing by the amps, her fingers on the sound knobs. She cuts off the noise and announces, "Now, are you all going to act like human beings, or do we end this rehearsal right now?"

Thank goodness <u>someone</u> is thinking.

No one's saying anything because our ears are ringing. I'm wondering if my eardrums have been pierced.

Then I hear James mutter, "sorry, guys."

He grabs his coat and heads out the door.

"Where are you going?" Rico calls out.

"Home," James replies.

I run out after him. Marina urges me to let him go. Maggie tries to call me back. But I don't listen to either of them.

I catch up to James, but he doesn't stop. He walks onto the sidewalk, fast.

"You can't <u>walk</u> home," I say. "It's too far."

James just grunts.

"James, what is <u>with</u> you? Why do you act like this?"

"I wouldn't if I didn't have to," he says through gritted teeth.

I tell him I was just sharing my day with everyone. I explain that I was feeling sad. I begin to describe what happened at GA≡A, but he cuts me off.

"Look," he says, "you can have bad days. Fine. But you make yourself so . . . _open_, Amalia. I mean, what would you do if I told every girl at vista all my problems?"

"It's not all my problems! I just — I mean, I can't help the way I feel — open is just how I am — and if someone wants to be nice to me — I mean, if it happened to you, so what?" (That's more or less it, Nbook. Something babbly and impossible to understand. You know me.)

Anyway, James is glaring at me, the way he was glaring at Justin. We're against the hedges of someone's house, and I can see no one else around.

James is changing before my eyes. Literally.

No, Nbook. He didn't hit me.
But he almost did.


I run back to Rico's. James
chases me, but when I reach the
garage, he's gone.
Justin and Rico are huddled over
some music equipment. Bruce and Patti
are talking with Mr. and Mrs. Chavez,
who have brought out some
refreshments.
Marina, Cece, Maggie, Dawn, Sunny,
and Ducky gather around me as I
walk in. They ask what happened, and
I tell them. Then I apologize to Ducky
for James's rude remarks.
"I've heard worse," Ducky says.
"Besides, _you_ shouldn't be the one
apologizing."
"Is he . . . coming back?" Maggie
asks.
"Who cares?" Sunny says.
"Sunny, he _is_ a big part of the
band," Dawn remarks.
"If he's going to be like that, I'd

rather we cancel the rehearsal,"
Maggie says.

"He gets hotheaded," I explain. "He
doesn't mean to act the way he does."

"You don't have to defend him,"
Bruce says.

"He has no right to talk to Justin
like that." That's Rico joining in. "Or
Ducky."

"Not to mention Amalia," Maggie
adds.

I still have this urge to explain
away James's behavior. But everyone
seems mad at him, and I can't
disagree.

All this time Marina is silent. I can
tell she's angry and upset but doesn't
want to speak up against her brother.

The rehearsal ends early. Maggie
offers me a ride home, which means
a chauffeur and a big car, so I say
yes.

As we pull away, Maggie looks
very concerned. I tell her what
happened — all of it. Maggie is quiet

For a second, thinking. Then she asks me what I'm going to do about James.

"I don't know," I say. "Call him, I guess. Try to figure him out."

Maggie is shaking her head. "Amalia, didn't you say he almost hit you?"

"Almost, but I got him angry. And he would never —"

"_Almost_ is too close. And it doesn't matter how angry you got him, Amalia. People aren't licensed to hit other people, for any reason."

"So what should I do?"

Maggie leans forward and takes my hand. "You really want to know what I think?"

"Yes."

"Break up with him. Now. The longer you wait, the sorrier you'll be."

"I _can't_ break up with him!"

"Why?"

"Because I'm not really going out with him!"

"So what's the problem?"

It's a good question, Nbook.
I don't know the answer.

Hallelujah. A sub today. I can sneak you in, Nbook.

News of the day: James is a mess.

The first time I see him is by the cafeteria door, before eighth-grade lunch. He's usually pretty grungy to begin with, but today he's worse than usual. His hair looks unwashed and he hasn't shaved.

I walk past him without saying a word. It's not that I _mean_ to ignore him. I'm just so afraid and guilty and confused, I don't know _what_ to say — and besides, I'm hoping he speaks first.

But he says nothing either. He just stares at me.

I grab a hot lunch. When I emerge from the lunch line, he's gone.

I sit with Cece and Marina. Marina tells me James didn't come home last night until after midnight. Soon Maggie and Dawn and Sunny are sitting with us. My fortress.

The count is unanimous. They all think I should break up with James — even Marina. (Add Isabel to the count too. Last night, when I told her what James had done, she freaked.)

Afterward, as we're all walking out of the cafeteria, James is at the door again. "Excuse me," he says softly. "Can I speak to you, Amalia?"

Sunny just continues gabbing, raising her voice as if she hasn't heard James at all. Everyone is pulling me along, away from him. I can't stop, even if I want to.

But he looks so sincere. So apologetic. As if he's about to cry.

I smile. "Later," I say over my shoulder.

I catch hell from Maggie for saying that.

But I do want to talk to him. He _is_ human.

## They found him!

Nbook, I am so _happy_.

I walk into the house after school today, feeling totally miserable, and the first thing that happens is my sister jumps on me.

Yes, dignified Saint Isabel. She's laughing and crying, and she says, "Ms. Hardwick just called. Mikey is all right!"

Well, I let out a scream, which makes Isabel scream even louder.

"The police found him with his dad in a fast-food place," Isabel explains. "Boy, is the dad in trouble. Linda had gotten a restraining order on him, which meant he wasn't legally allowed to go near Linda in the first place. Plus, Linda has legal custody of Mikey. So the police are holding the father in jail, and they returned Mikey to Linda."

"Can we visit them now?" I ask.

Isabel's face droops. "Tomorrow. Ms. Hardwick says we should give them time to be alone together."

I groan and throw my book bag on the living room sofa.

As I slump inside, I notice the answering machine ticker reads 5.

I press the playback button. The voice on Message 1 is immediately familiar: "This is for Amalia. When she gets in, could she please call James?"

Message 2: "Hi, James again. Just thought you might be in."

Message 3 was a hang-up.

Message 4: "Hey, it's Rico, for Amalia. Listen, rehearsal's canceled for tonight. I think we should all chill for a week, okay? See you."

Message 5: "Hello, it's James.... Anybody there? I know you're probably home by now ... hmm, maybe

you went shopping or something. . . .
Hello? Amalia?" <u>Click</u>.

Isabel looked disgusted. "Speaking of abusive men."

"He's not a man," I say. "And he's not abusive."

"Oh? What do <u>you</u> call it when someone raises a hand to you?"

"Come on, Isabel. <u>You've</u> done that to me. Should I call the police on you?"

"Don't be blind, sister. Everyone sees the truth but you. Tell me you are going to dump this guy."

"Maybe I will. Maybe not. It's my life, Isabel."

"That's what all of them say at GAEA. And look what ends up happening."

My mouth clanks open. "You're comparing <u>James</u> to <u>Robert</u>, that — that horrible monster? How could you?"

Isabel just snorts in disgust and walks away.

And now I'm sitting at the kitchen table. I should go up to Mami and Papi's room and call James. But right now I'm feeling a little chicken.

I don't know what I'll say to him.

Everyone else thinks this is so easy. "Hi. You're a jerk. I never want to see you again."

But I can't do it. At least not like that.

James is not evil, Nbook. He's trying. He deserves to have a chance.

So I'll listen to what he has to say. Then maybe I'll know what to do.

Okay, here goes. I will let you know what happens right away.

Sat 1/10
9:30 A.M.

Sorry, Nbook. I lied.

But I couldn't help it. I was in no condition to write last night.

I am scared.

I feel like I'm living in a nightmare that gets worse and worse the more I try to wake up.

I keep thinking of all the ifs that could have happened. If rehearsal hadn't been canceled. If Ms. Hardwick had allowed Isabel and me to visit Linda. If Mami and Papi had been in a bad mood and forced me to stay home.

If any of those things had occurred, last night would have been just fine.

Slow down, Amalia.

Take it from the top.

Yesterday afternoon, just as I'm heading upstairs to call James, Mami and Papi come home from work.

It's Papi and Isabel's turn to prepare dinner, so I finally run upstairs.

I tap out James's phone number. He picks up on the first ring. His voice is soft and almost formal.

"Hello, Amalia," he says. "Thanks for calling back."

"What's up?"

"I was wondering if we could meet. Now that rehearsal has been canceled, I'm free. You?"

"Uh, sure. Want to come over?"

"I thought the Firehouse Cafe might be a better idea. I'll pick you up — I mean, if you want."

I check with Mami and Papi. Mami says I need to have dinner with the family. Papi says it's okay to go out afterward, now that the kidnapper has been caught.

"After dinner, James," I reply.

"Is 7:30 okay?"

"Uh-huh."

"I could wait longer."

"No. 7:30's great."

We say good-bye. I'm kind of touched. I can tell James is trying hard to be considerate.

After dinner I dress up. James arrives exactly on time. He is actually wearing beautiful clothes. He's shaved, and his hair is pulled into a ponytail. I can tell he's showered, because the hair is still wet. And he makes a point of getting out of the car and opening the passenger door for me.

I have never seen a guy do that in Palo City.

We listen to music on the way. We talk. Neither of us mentions what happened Thursday night.

It is my first time going to the Firehouse Cafe. It really is a converted firehouse, with exposed brick walls and high-backed booths. Lots of privacy.

We sit in the back and order food. (I order dessert, since I already had dinner.)

We're alone now. I'm looking into James's eyes, but he's staring into his water glass.

"You're being nice to me today," I say.

"I'm trying," James mumbles.

"Well, I like that. It's a start."

"I —" James's voice cracks. He clears his throat. "Sometimes I don't understand why you even want to see me."

"Sometimes I don't either."

I mean that to sound lighthearted, but it comes out harsher than I expect.

But James isn't offended. In fact, he's nodding. "I'm a total jerk, Amalia. I don't deserve you. I don't deserve any girlfriend."

"Hey, don't go overboard —"

"It's true. If you were to tell me right now, 'James, this is it. I never want to see you again' — if you were to throw that glass of water in my face and walk out, I wouldn't blame you."

"I'm not going to do that!"

Now James looks me in the eye. "You're not?"

"Well, not the glass part."

"But you want to break up?"

"I — we haven't — maybe if we —" I stammer.

"Tell me, Amalia. Because right now I feel like —" James cuts himself off. He takes a long swig from his water glass.

"You feel like what?" I ask.

James swallows hard. He looks off into the distance, his eyes glassy. "I've been having a rough time. It's not only you and me. But the group, school, stuff at home . . ."

I'm thinking: Vanish is doing great, James has decent grades in school, and he has never complained about his family before. "Did something happen?" I ask.

"Not _bad_ bad, like a death or anything. Just . . . pressure. It's, like, _life_ things, you know? Anyway, you were the only good thing happening to me. I mean, did I think I would like an _eighth-grader_ more than anyone else I ever met? No way. But look what happened. And now — now I've messed that up too."

"Look, James, you don't have to be so hard on yourself. We can talk this out —"

"Hard on myself — that's exactly it!

See, you know my mind, Amalia. Even though you're only 13. It's, like, you could be a senior or something. I <u>need</u> people to understand me. <u>No one</u> does. All the ideas in my head, the creative stuff, the music and all — it's, like, a different world in there. I can't even talk to people about it. I can express it only in my guitar playing, you know? But when I met you, I said, 'Wow. She knows. She can see.'"

"You never told me you felt that way, James."

James leans forward. "I've gone out with a lot of girls, Amalia. I know what I need. You're, like, <u>it</u>. Which is why I can't lose you, Amalia. It's like that old song, 'I can't live if livin' is without you.' That's what I feel."

I don't know how to take this. For some reason, I can't help laughing. Not to make fun of him, but because he's making me nervous. "You couldn't live without me?"

Right away I know I've reacted the wrong way. James is angry. His eyes have that same look they had on Thursday night. "Why am I spilling out my guts to you? Do you understand this language? Or are you just acting stupid?"

The urge to laugh is way gone. A block of ice is forming in my stomach, and it's spreading all over my body. "I do understand the language," I say. "But I don't understand you. You _just_ said that I'm the only person who _does_ understand you, and now you say I don't understand you —"

"Do you know how many people I show my feelings to? Nobody! And you're just acting like it means nothing. So I have to deal with my anger with all these people around, hearing me, while you sit here eating a free meal —"

That does it. I stand up from the table.

"I do not have to be treated like this, James. I've listened enough to how you feel. You want to know how _I_ feel? I'll tell you. You care about one thing — yourself. You don't have the slightest idea who I am."

"But I'm sure you're going to let me know," James says sarcastically.

"No," I reply. "Because I don't ever want to see you again. There. Do you understand <u>that</u> language?"

People in the cafe are staring at us now. James is rising. His fists are clenched, but I don't care.

I turn and walk away.

James grabs my arm. "Wait. Your house is too far away. You can't walk there."

"Oh no? Watch me."

"Don't. Please don't. I'm sorry. I'm so sorry." James is pulling me back with both arms now. His voice sounds tender and bruised.

My body plops down in the seat. But my mind is heading out the door.

James's face is beet red. His lips are quivering. "I did it again. I blew it again — <u>I am such a stupid idiot!</u>"

I say nothing. I feel nothing. He

can yell at himself, he can apologize, it doesn't matter.

"Okay," James says softly, trying to compose himself, "I will say it plainly. I need you. If I can't have you, Amalia, say good-bye to me forever. I will die."

Sorry, Nbook. I had to take a break. This is hard for me to write about.

When James says that thing about dying, I start feeling sick. I tell him I need to go home.

He pays the check and drives me back. This is our car ride:

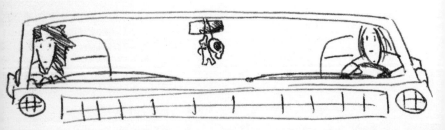

James is trying to make conversation about music and school and our friends. As if nothing weird has happened.

Me? I am in shock. I am convinced he is a total maniac.

But he drives me home safely. Maybe he makes a move to kiss me good-bye, but I wouldn't know. I'm out that passenger door the moment the car stops.

Mami and Papi are watching TV when I walk in. Isabel's out with Simon. I say hello, go straight to my room, and crash.

Now, I wish I could say that's that and James is out of my life.

But later that night the phone rings, and I hear Mami saying, "Hello, James."

When she comes up to my room, I pretend I'm fast asleep.

And this morning, I wake up to find a message from him on the answering machine and then four hang-ups.

Over breakfast I tell Mami, Papi,

and Isabel that James and I have broken up. I keep the details to a minimum, but I make it clear that I don't want to talk to him.

Today James has called <u>3 more times</u>. Luckily, I've been out of the house.

I don't know what is going to happen.

I can't let him think that I still want to go out with him. But how can I break up after what he told me?

What if he's serious?

Okay. I have to calm down. I have to stop thinking about this.

1/1∅
5:3∅ P.M.

I can't.

I can't let it go.

Isabel asks me to run some errands, and I figure that'll keep my mind off James. So what do I talk about in the car? James.

I tell her everything. And she says two things that blow me away.

First she says that James has an inferiority complex.

Yes, _inferiority_.

He feels inferior _inside_, so he needs someone on the _outside_ to tell him how talented and wonderful he is. To him, I'm like a young, worshipping little doll. So when I show a mind of my own, he can't take it.

Which makes sense, when you think about it. But then comes the worst part.

Isabel says that _I_ do the same thing, in a way. I make _James_ into something he isn't.

"No way, Isabel. I see him _exactly_ the way he is."

"Now you do. You didn't at first."

I tell her she's crazy. But inside I know she's not. When I first met James, what was I seeing? Not him, really. To me, he was <u>somebody</u>. I was feeling so insecure, this brand-new helpless eighth-grader. But when I walked down the hall with him at vista, I was somebody too. He was cool. So was I.

All these thoughts are swirling through my head as Isabel and I pull up to the front of the house.

James's car is parked in front.

And he's inside it.

"Uh-oh," Isabel mutters.

"Ignore him," I say.

We park in the garage. As we get out of the car, James is walking toward us. He's holding a bouquet of flowers.

He says hi. I say hi.

"Can I talk to you a minute?" he asks.

"Get lost," Isabel says.

She pulls me into the house before I can take the flowers. James stands there, watching.

A few minutes later I'm up in my

bedroom. I peek out the window and he's still there.

I duck under the windowsill. I want to tell Isabel, but I feel frozen. Maybe he's seen me. If I stand up, he'll know for sure.

I must be down there, huddled on my bed, for ten minutes. When I finally have the courage to look back out the window, he's gone.

I've been up here ever since
The phone just rang.
I know it's him. He won't stop.
What is happening to me?

Sun 1/11
7:10 A.M.

Well, looks like you survived the night just fine, Nbook. Wish I could say the same about myself.

The phone call last night? I'll give you 3 guesses who it was from, and the first 2 don't count.

"Amaliaaaaaa!" Mami calls upstairs. "It's James."

I debate hanging up on him. Now I wish I had.

But I pick up the receiver in Mami and Papi's room and say hello.

You will never believe what he says.

"Hey, Amalia. want to go out tonight?"

Like we've been flung into a time warp and the Firehouse Cafe never happened.

"James, you —" <u>are a total ignorant jerk</u>, is what I should say. But all that comes out of my mouth is, "No. I can't."

"Tomorrow, then?"

Now Isabel is peeking into the room. She holds out a clenched fist, as if to say, <u>Stand firm</u>. I frown and wave her away.

"No, James," I say. "I can't then either."

"Tuesday?"

"I — look, we — no." I close my eyes and count to five slowly. "Not Tuesday, not Wednesday, not any day."

"Just to talk. As a friend, that's all. I have to show you something."

"No, James—"

"Look. If Maggie asked you to go out, you would, right?"

"That's different."

"Right. She's a girl. Okay, <u>Justin</u>, say."

"James, I am hanging up now—"

"Look, I have to see you. I'll drive over. It'll take a few minutes—"

"No. Stay home. Good-bye."

James starts saying something, but I'm already hanging up.

As soon as the receiver clacks into the cradle, I hear Isabel whooping from outside the bedroom door.

"Eavesdropper," I say.

Isabel stands in the doorway and smiles. "I'm proud of you."

<u>Bleeeeeeeeeep</u>, goes the phone.

"DON'T ANSWER!" I shout to Mami and Papi downstairs.

It keeps bleeping. Isabel and I run downstairs to the answering machine.

It clicks on.

"Hello?" says James's voice. Then, "I know you're listening."

Isabel and I look at each other. We're both gulping. I reach for the receiver, but she grabs my wrist.

"No one treats me like this, Amalia," the voice says. "I am bending over backward to give you a chance. Pick up now or you will regret it."

I feel like I am going to throw up.

Isabel is holding onto my arm. I shake loose, but I don't reach for the phone.

We hear a click. The answering machine cuts off.

Now Mami is standing behind us. "What are you girls doing?" she asks.

Isabel shrugs. "It was a crank call."

Well, Nbook, that is all I heard from James. No more calls the rest of the day.

I try not to think about what he said at the Firehouse. About dying. But it's not like him to avoid calling me, and I'm worried that he might try to

Well, I don't even want to mention it.

But this morning, around 1:00, the phone wakes me up. I hear Papi's groggy voice saying, "Hello . . . ? Hello . . . ?" Then I hear the receiver crashing back into the cradle, while Papi mutters something not too nice about a hang-up.

No one answers the call at 3:20. Everyone's fast asleep and can't hear it. Except me.

I have big trouble going back to sleep after that. When I do, I keep <u>dreaming</u> that the phone is ringing.

I'm totally awake now. Might as well start the day. It's gorgeous outside. Looks like it might be hot enough for

What is that thing on the lawn?

Don't go away, Nbook. I'll be right back.

This is not happening.
This is just too weird.
The thing on the lawn? It's two things. Two old rag dolls, a boy and a girl. They're in a pile, and I pull them apart. This is what they look like:

Should I wake Isabel?
I have to talk to somebody.
I am shaking.

Okay. I just called Maggie. She's a morning person. She was up.

She says that this kind of thing happened in one of her dad's films. I should ignore it. Calling James would be doing just what he <u>wants</u> me to do.

Most of all, I should not act scared or look scared.

Right.

Isabel thinks Maggie is crazy. "Living in La-La Land," is how she puts it. She thinks I should call the police right away.

Mami and Papi weigh in.

Mami says, "Even though it may seem obvious, you're still not positive he did this." She thinks I should invite him over, with the whole family in the house. I should have the two dolls sitting on the coffee table, and I should make <u>no comment</u>. Let him do the talking.

Papi wants to talk to James himself.

I can't tell which of those ideas is worse.

<u>What should I do?</u>

11:21

The phone rings. I'm curled up in bed.

Papi answers it with the loudest, most unfriendly "Hello" I've ever heard.

Then, "Amalia! It's for you!"

It's Maggie. Inviting me over to chill. Dawn and Sunny will be there too.

I am out of here, Nbook.

Back again.

I love my Palo City friends.

We're sitting around the pool, eating nachos, trying not to be too freaked about James. And you know what Maggie tells me? She says Rico has called up James and read him the riot act.

Bruce and Patti are mad at him too.

I'm almost in tears when I hear this. I'm amazed that they're loyal to <u>me</u>. James has been with the group since the beginning.

That was the first good thing that happened. The next? When Papi picked up the phone and threatened him. Exactly how? Neither he nor Mami will tell me.

But he did not call back.

I have hope, Nbook.

Maybe I'll sleep tonight. Wish me luck.

I did it.

Slept right through the night.

And there were no calls overnight.

I'm looking out my window. Nothing on the lawn.

Maybe it's over.

No. I can't let myself be overoptimistic.

I still have to get through the entire school day.

I am not singing hallelujahs yet.

But the signs are good.

I see James in the hallway on my way here. He's with his friends. They all smile at me. James waves.

That's it. He doesn't come after me. He just stays put.

I'll check back after lunch.

I'm early. Waiting for friends to arrive.

James is not at the doorway today. I am feeling more and more

Sorry, Nbook. Gotta move. Girls at the next table are being snots. Looking at me, whispering and laughing.

Haven't they ever seen someone write in a journal before?

Where do I begin?

Nbook, I am in shock.

You know what those girls were laughing at? Graffiti on the cafeteria wall.

Graffiti that looked something like this:

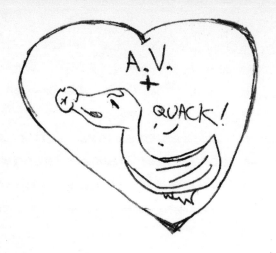

I go right to the head custodian,
and he's in there with stain remover
in seconds.

But you can still see it.

Sunny is practically in tears when
she arrives at the table. She says
everyone in school is talking about
Ducky and me. There's this rumor
"from an eyewitness" that I've been
chasing him. That I forced him to kiss
me behind Rico's garage at a vanish
rehearsal.

Then Maggie comes to the table.

She's upset because some kids in her math class have heard that I fooled around with Justin.

She makes it clear that she doesn't believe it. She's just upset anyone would think it.

Marina just ignores me. She and Cece sit at another table. Is she feeling guilty? Angry? What's going on?

I am fed up. After lunch I wait for James.

He comes strolling down the hallway. I ask him if he wrote the graffiti on the wall.

He asks, "What graffiti?"

When I show him he just shrugs and says, "You and Ducky? Who would even imagine such a ridiculous thing? Too bad you're not still going out with me. Then no one would even suspect it was true."

I want to scream at him. I want to kill him.

But the words get stuck in my throat. And he walks out of the building.

# THE RESCUE OF AMALIA

When I ask Mami and Papi about going to Rico's, they seem cautious. Papi still thinks James is a dangerous psycho. Mami worries about what Rico said. To her, "solve your problem" could mean something threatening, like a fight.

Isabel to the rescue. She insists on going along. She promises to whisk me away if anything bad happens.

Fine with Mami and Papi. Fine with me.

Isabel drives me to Rico's. Everyone's there. Except James.

Right off the bat, Isabel asks if this is a revenge meeting.

Rico shakes his head. "It's a <u>strategy</u> meeting. Family strategy. That's how I see Vanish. Either we stick together as a family, or . . ."

"We vanish," Bruce remarks.

"But James is a part of the family too," I say. "He's an original member. He brought <u>me</u> in."

"You're our manager," Patti speaks up. "We're all equal."

"I think we ought to talk to him," Rico says. "Let him explain himself — why he started those rumors, why he's treating Amalia so badly —"

"He's been acting like a jerk for too long," Bruce cuts in. "We don't need him. Kick him out."

"That's what I say!" Maggie blurts out.

"Be fair," Patti says. "I agree with Rico. Let's call him now and ask him to come over."

Everyone (except Maggie and me) is mumbling in agreement.

"Don't bother. He's here."

The voice comes from the garage door. It makes me freeze up inside.

It's James.

He strolls through the garage door. Smiling.

It's that evil smile of his. Right away I know he's heard the conversation.

No one speaks. We're all too shocked.

"What's the matter?" James asks. "You only kick people out behind their backs?"

Rico steps forward. "We're not doing that. We wanted you to explain yourself first —"

"And _then_ you'll kick me out." James is glaring at Bruce. "That's the thanks I get for bringing you into this group, even though you can't play?"

Bruce turns red. He starts sputtering. But James is moving on to Maggie now.

"And you," he says. "You think you'd have gotten into this group if my sister hadn't begged me —"

"Shut up, James!" Patti blurts out.

"You're killing it for yourself, man," Rico adds. "We wanted to give you a chance —"

James laughs. He says he doesn't need the group. He says we're all a bunch of tone-deaf amateurs. He turns away and calls out, "Come on, Amalia."

<u>Come on, Amalia!</u> I'm supposed to follow after him like a little chihuahua?

I want to throw something at him.

I'm about to yell, but Isabel beats me to it. "Don't you talk to her like that," she says.

"Oh, I'm scared," James replies, laughing. "Big sister's going to beat me up."

"Big sister and friends," Bruce says through clenched teeth.

"Hit me with the bass," James remarks. "You might make a decent sound for once."

That does it.

Bruce is ready to fight.

Maggie is in tears.

Patti is furious.

Rico is telling James never to set foot in his garage again.

And I'm ready to kill him.

Rico, Bruce, and Patti are advancing on James. His eyes are on me. I see fear in them. But I also see mockery. And anger.

"You have a lot of people fighting your battles, Amalia!" James shouts scornfully.

I'm thinking, this may be the first and last time I am agreeing with James Kodaly.

This is not Maggie's battle. Or Isabel's. Or Rico's.

It's mine.

Suddenly Bruce lunges. James ducks aside and holds up his fists.

"Knock it off!" I shout.

Both guys turn toward me. Bruce mumbles something under his breath and backs off.

I am facing James now. His features are tense, almost distorted. It's amazing how someone so handsome can make himself look so ugly.

I feel drained. I feel empty. But I don't feel scared.

"James," I say. "You don't need to start rumors about me. Because no one will believe you. You don't need to pick fights. Because even if you beat someone up, you can't change anything. And you don't need me. Because I will never be your stuffed animal."

James is looking at me as if I'm a small, annoying child. "This all happened because of me," I continue. "Because I was stupid enough to trust you. But I'm not making that mistake anymore."

I look James in the eye. I wait for him to react.

When he doesn't, I turn away. "Let's get out of here," I say.

I walk out of the garage and toward the car. To my surprise, everyone else is following me.

Including James.

"Wait," he calls out.

I look back. Some of the others don't.

"You're right," James says. "I'm sorry. I did the wrong thing. I really, really lost it."

I nod. Isabel and I climb into the car.

"Yeah," I say out the window. "You did."

Nbook, I can't believe five days have passed since I last wrote.

My excuse? Homework, I guess. Exhaustion.

Also, I'm so tired of bad news. And the week is full of it. I guess I just don't want to depress you.

But I feel the urge to write again, Nbook. Hope you don't mind.

First I'll let Linda's card speak for itself.

Dear Isabel,

I hope you can come visit Mikey and me before we move. You've been like a younger sister to me.

Robert has been released. Despite the fact that he violated the restraining order. Despite the fact that he trespassed on GAEA's property. And despite the fact that he kidnapped Mikey. He's under surveillance, and he's wearing some kind of electronic monitoring device.

I am going to have to testify against him in court. In the meantime I am sending Mikey away to a place where I know he'll be happy and safe. And I will be living with some people I know.

Please come see us so we can say good-bye.

Love,
Linda
and
MIKEY

The only positive thing I can say, Nbook, is that Mikey seemed really happy when we visited.

But as of Wednesday, he and Linda are in places where no one can find them.

I search the newspapers every day for reports of Linda's case. But I haven't read anything that resembles it.

I know I may not ever see them again, Nbook. But that doesn't keep me from thinking about them. All the time.

I just read over the last entry. I realize it's the first time in awhile I haven't written about James.

Guess you've been wondering what's been happening between him and me, huh, Nbook?

Well, until today, nothing.

I see him from time to time in school. We don't ignore each other or stare menacingly. Sometimes we just nod. Once or twice we've said "Hi."

I don't know how he's feeling. Marina doesn't say much. I think she feels caught in the middle. Our friendship has definitely taken a nosedive.

As for Vanish, well, we haven't met for rehearsal. I know I should call Rico, and I will, eventually. Maggie thinks he's totally lost interest in the group.

Mami, Papi, and Isabel are glad James is not calling. Simon is hinting I should meet his ninth-grade brother, who's even dorkier than Simon.

One good thing about all this — it's brought me closer to Maggie and her friends. I like them all so much.

Actually, not counting what happened to Linda and Mikey, things have been going pretty well.

Until today.

Vista's having this Valentine's Day bake sale, to raise funds for gym repairs. I first see the sign-up sheet after second period, and I sign my name on the second-to-last slot under Decorations Committee. On the way to third period I see Maggie and ask her to sign the last slot.

Later she tells me she did just that. But when the committees are announced later, her name isn't mentioned. James's is.

I corner him after school and ask about this.

But he's with a group of new friends and he just shrugs.

I head to my locker, furious. I pull it open and a note floats to the floor.

DIDN'T I TELL YOU WE WERE
MEANT FOR EACH OTHER?
XXXOOO
GUESS
WHO

**Ann M. Martin**

# About the Author

ANN MATTHEWS MARTIN was born on August 12, 1955. She grew up in Princeton, NJ, with her parents and her younger sister, Jane.

Although Ann used to be a teacher and then an editor of children's books, she's now a full-time writer. She gets the ideas for her books from many different places. Some are based on personal experiences. Others are based on childhood memories and feelings. Many are written about contemporary problems or events.

All of Ann's characters are made up. But some of her characters are based on real people. Sometimes Ann names her characters after people she knows; other times she chooses names she likes.

In addition to California Diaries, Ann Martin has written many other books, including the Baby-sitters Club series. She has written twelve novels for young people, including *Missing Since Monday, With You or Without You, Slam Book,* and *Just a Summer Romance.*

Ann M. Martin does not live in California, though she does visit frequently. She lives in New York with her cats, Gussie and Woody. Her hobbies are reading, sewing, and needlework — especially making clothes for children.

He's there. And he's all smiles.

"It's the Duckster! Duckopolis! Duckman! Duckorama!

Slap. Slap. Slap. Slap. That's what each of those stupid names feels like.

He says right out: He was just over your house, and you were out -- which makes you gulp.

Then he says he has to show you something.